Woodall Media

Words go away

"Get out! GET OUT!!!
I just don't care..."
His mother's words cut through the air.

"You take the boy and leave!"
Father steamed as he screamed.

A broken record that played
day after day.
He closed his eyes, but the words
never went away.
He knew he needed to escape.

The sun set, and he locked his door.
He made his bed once more.

He twisted the handle and heard a noise,
A howl; he scowled, perhaps his toys.

Quietly, he tiptoed into the darkness where he found:

A new world.
A small,
dark town.

Running across a still dirt road,
he sped by barns and farms,

Where animals dozed.

He passed cows and pigs
and chickens and more...

He kept running until stumbling upon another, bigger door.

And in that door,
which he pushed open:
waves of wings—
a humid black ocean.

Creatures flooded overhead,
full of commotion.

Squawks and squeals and piercing shrills.
He glanced up to a blurry black world.

Then on his shoulder, landed a small bat, with a head that twisted across its back.

He smiled at his new friend,
who nodded and said,
"You've found the end."

Suddenly, with a quick prick,
the bat squeaked,

sinking its teeth into his cheek.

"You'll be one of us within a week!"

The boy felt sick and his heart thumped.
What did the bat mean?

He was
stumped.

But then, in his throat grew a lump, and on his face, tiny rough bumps.

His teeth became sharp
and he grew hungry.
He searched his pockets,
But they were all empty.

The bat smiled, "Come with me."
The boy's eyes glazed over,
"But I cannot see!"

"NO, no. HEAR
with your ears;
Listen for the squeeeaks!"

The bat cackled in a high-pitched cheer.

The boy, BOY could he hear!

He heard it all, and in his mind,
A picture of the world, sharp and bright.

Better than the ONE
that he left behind.

So he stretched his arms
and began to fly.

He whooped and whistled,
screamed and cried,
following the colony
on their nightly ride.

They landed
on the backs
of sheep and cows,
digging their teeth into their chow.

The boy's stomach gurgled and snarled at him. Instinct had begun to kick in.

He found the biggest heifer
and landed on her back.
His teeth were big. and sharp,
He needed a snack.

So he clamped down on her hide,
ripping her flesh.
The taste of blood, so heavy so fresh.

He made his way back,
with his new friends.
All full, and merry, and drunk.

And the bat whispered,
"Never again will you be alone
We were like you long ago.
We escaped too and found this town.
Now let us rest, no more frowns."

So the boy closed his eyes,
with peace and comfort
and love and friends,

For the first time in his life.

riTten bye
Kenneth Woodall

Pro-Duck-chin Coredinatur/
Storeybored Rtist
Steve Lonberger

illuhstraytehr
Ilja Wegner

www.ingramcontent.com/pod-product-compliance
Lightning Source LLC
Chambersburg PA
CBHW041540240626
47164CB00002B/78